Ankylosaurus
The clumsy club

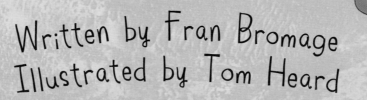

Written by Fran Bromage
Illustrated by Tom Heard

MiLes
KeLLy

Once upon a time there was an Ankylosaurus called Archie.

Archie was a **tough-looking** dinosaur, but he was ever so shy and ever so **clumsy**.

Archie had a **huge club**
at the end of his tail.

It seemed to do the
exact opposite of what
he wanted it to do.

When Archie walked, his club **swiped** from side to side.

He often **destroyed** things just by wandering past them.

So Archie spent a lot of time saying **SORRY** to other dinosaurs.

His club was always getting him into trouble.

WHOOOOSH!

"Watch your club!" grumbled an old Edmontonia. "I don't know why you've got one, if you can't control it."

Archie's best friend was a Styracosaurus called Stu.

But even with Stu about Archie was still **left out** of games.

"Stu! Come and play hide and seek," shouted an Ornithomimus called Olivia, one afternoon.

"HE can't play though," added Olivia, pointing to Archie. "He'll **knock** half the forest down before we've had time to hide."

It made Archie feel sad, but he told Stu to go and play anyway.

Archie stood and watched as all the other dinosaurs ran off to hide.

"Can I at least help you find them?" Archie asked Olivia, as he lumbered up to her.

"...18, 19, 20. Coming!" she shouted. "Oh, I suppose so," she replied, "just try to be quiet."

But suddenly Archie
spotted a dinosaur who
wasn't part of the game.
"Olivia!" he shouted.

"Ssssh!" she replied crossly.
"T. REX!" hissed Archie.

"T. REEEEEX!"
shrieked Olivia, as
she **overtook** Archie
and sped toward a
nearby cave.

Archie could see the
other dinosaurs already
hiding in the cave.

Stu was waiting for him, but was Archie going to get there in time?

Suddenly there was a **thundering roar** and the ground began to shake.

Archie wondered what he'd hit with his club this time. But when he looked behind him the sky was filling with smoke.

As the volcano shot
fiery balls of lava into
the air, Archie still
hadn't reached the cave.

Everyone else ducked
inside just as a
rumbling rockfall filled
the cave entrance.

Archie huddled close
to the cave. As the
eruption finished he started
pushing at the rocks.

"I can't shift
any of them,"
he grunted.

"Try harder!" shouted Stu from inside the cave.
"We can only move the **little ones** in here."

Olivia **squeezed** her **head** into the small gap Stu was making.

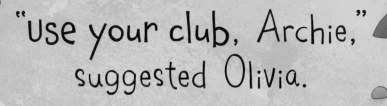

"Use your club, Archie," suggested Olivia.

"I'll hurt someone," said Archie. "I always **break** something with it."

"Hurry Archie!" shouted Olivia. "T. rex is back!"

"Just give your tail a swish and try. Please?" called Stu. So Archie **started to spin**...

Archie's club **slammed** into the fallen rocks. Small trees and boulders were caught up in his whirling and T. rex was **knocked out** cold!

As Archie slowed to a stop, he saw the rocks around the cave had shifted.

"Well done Archie!" shouted the dinosaurs from inside the cave.

"Thanks Archie," whispered each dinosaur as they **tiptoed over** T. rex to leave the cave.

"You took on a T. rex with your tail?" whispered a small Edmontonia. "Amazing!"

Archie suddenly felt very proud of his club.

Archie was soon part of everyone's games and found he was especially good at rock-ball! "Archie's club is awesome!" laughed Olivia.